The Journey of Restoration

Rediscovering Hope in the Midst of Chaos

ERIC COOPER

Above the Sun Consultant Group Inc.

Preface

Welcome to " ***The Journey of Restoration: Rediscovering Hope in the Midst of Chaos***," a profound exploration of faith, resilience, and the enduring power of redemption. Within the pages of this captivating allegory, you will embark on a spiritual odyssey that transcends time and space, guiding you through the trials and triumphs of characters whose stories mirror our own.

As you immerse yourself in the narrative, prepare to be transported to the heart of **Sotira City**[1], a city teeming with turmoil and hope. Through the eyes of ***Eli***[2] *and* ***Jeremiah***[3], our protagonists, you will witness the raw beauty of human vulnerability, the depths of despair, and the unyielding resilience of the human spirit.

But beyond mere storytelling, "***The Journey of Restoration***" is an invitation—a call to embrace your own journey of self-discovery and spiritual growth. As you walk alongside our characters, may their experiences serve as mirrors reflecting the challenges and triumphs of your own life.

In the midst of chaos and uncertainty, let this allegory be a guiding light, illuminating the path to healing, forgiveness, and ultimate restoration. May it inspire you to embark on a journey of faith and transformation where the transformative power of God's love knows no bounds.

Prepare to be captivated, challenged, and ultimately uplifted as you embark on "***The Journey of Restoration,***" a voyage of the soul that promises to leave an indelible mark on your heart and spirit.

The Journey of Restoration— Rediscovering Hope in the Midst of Chaos

For more information or to book an event, contact:

contact@abovethesun.ca or abovethesun.ca

Book design & Cover design by Above the Sun Consultant Group Inc.

ASIN E-Book: B0D1NYQXVW
ASIN Paperback: 1738279898
ASIN Hardcover: 1068820004
ISBN: Paperback: 978-1-7382798-9-0
ISBN: Hardcover : 978-1-0688200-0-7

amazon.ca/dp/B0D1NYQXVW
amazon.com/dp/B0D1NYQXVW
amazon.com/author/abovethesun

First Edition: May 2024

Dedication

To all those who have faced seemingly insurmountable challenges, who find themselves amidst the wreckage of broken dreams and shattered hopes, and who yearn for the light of restoration to pierce through the darkness.

This book is dedicated to you— the courageous souls who refuse to surrender to despair, who cling to hope amidst the storm, and who believe in the possibility of a brighter tomorrow.

Whether you are navigating the aftermath of a devastating loss, battling against the forces of injustice and oppression, or simply seeking solace in a world filled with chaos and confusion, may you find inspiration, encouragement, and, above all, hope within these pages.

May the journey of our characters serve as a beacon of light in your darkest hour, guiding you towards the promise of redemption that awaits on the horizon.

With heartfelt solidarity and unwavering support,

Eric D. Cooper, Author, Visionary and Seeker of Truth
EricCooper.com

Contents

Introduction

In a world shrouded in darkness and uncertainty, where chaos reigns and hope seem but a distant dream, there exists a glimmer of light—a beacon of hope that pierces through the shadows, illuminating the path to redemption.

Welcome to ***"The Journey of Restoration: Rediscovering Hope in the Midst of Chaos"*** a captivating tale of faith, courage, and the transformative power of love. Set in the bustling city of **Sotira City**[1], this epic adventure follows the journey of **Eli**[2], a young entrepreneur, and his wise mentor **Jeremiah**[3], as they navigate the trials and tribulations of life in search of truth, justice, and ultimately, redemption.

From the devastating aftermath of a hurricane that leaves Eli's world in ruins to the seductive allure of wealth and power that threatens to ensnare his soul, each chapter of this gripping allegory takes readers on a rollercoaster ride of emotions. Suspense, intrigue, and heartwarming moments of compassion and grace are interwoven seamlessly, drawing readers deeper into the story with each turn of the page.

Inspired by timeless Biblical truths and real-world experiences, ***"The Journey of Restoration"*** invites readers to embark on a transformative journey of self-discovery and spiritual growth. As they accompany Eli and Jeremiah on their quest for meaning and purpose in a world filled with chaos and confusion, readers will find themselves confronted with profound truths and life-changing insights.

Through the trials and triumphs of its characters, this book serves as a powerful reminder that even in the darkest of times, hope endures for those who dare to seek the *Light of the world*. It is a story of resilience in the face of adversity, of forgiveness in the midst of pain, and of the unwavering power of faith to overcome even the greatest of challenges.

Get ready to experience a journey of a lifetime with ***"The Journey of Restoration"*** - a heartwarming adventure that will take you on a rollercoaster ride of emotions. As you take each step forward, you'll be captivated by the fascinating story that will lead you to the ultimate redemption. So, fasten your seatbelts and brace yourself for an unforgettable experience that will touch your heart and soul.

Chapter 1: The Valley of Lamentation

In the throbbing heart of **Sotira City**[1], where skyscrapers clawed at the heavens and streets thrummed with ceaseless activity, lay a small suburban sanctuary where **Eli**[2], a determined young entrepreneur, had set his roots. With unwavering determination, he had cultivated his business from a mere seedling to a burgeoning enterprise. Success shimmered on the horizon, tantalizingly close—until calamity descended with the fury of **Hurricane Redemption**.

As the sun dipped low, painting long, somber shadows across the streets of *Sotira City*, Eli stood framed in his doorway. The weight of his world seemed to converge upon his shoulders, a ponderous burden that threatened to crush him. The laughter and vibrancy that once filled this neighborhood had evaporated, replaced by a haunting silence that spoke of profound loss.

Hurricane Redemption tore through the city with relentless savagery, leaving behind a swath of destruction where Eli's home stood defenseless. As tempestuous winds roared and relentless rains lashed, Eli's world was dismantled around him, piece by piece. Amidst the uproar, his heart clenched with dread as he scoured the chaos for his family.

Days bled into each other as Eli traversed the wreckage of what once was a testament to his dreams. The landscape of his life lay in ruins, and the heavens above seemed deaf to his pleas for solace. The once bright future was now shrouded in shadows of doubt and the silence of **Yahweh**[8]. Each broken beam and shattered window in his home was a piercing reminder of the vibrant life that had flourished there—now just echoes in the void.

Eli was standing in the middle of an empty room, his eyes red and puffy, and his face contorted with anguish. Tears were streaming down his face, leaving moist trails on his cheeks, as he cried out in despair. His voice was hoarse and choked with emotion, as he expressed his pain and frustration to the heavens. *"How long, O Lord? Will You forget me forever? Why do You hide Your face from me in my hour of greatest need?"* He felt like he was all alone in the world, with no one to turn to in his moment of crisis.

The weight of his grief was overwhelming, and he struggled to find any semblance of hope or comfort. Each passing moment felt like an eternity as he waited for a response, hoping that someone, anyone in heaven, would hear his plea and offer him solace.

Yet, the response was only the deepening of twilight into darkness, deepening Eli's isolation. However, a faint spark of hope flickered defiantly in the abyss of his despair. This ember, resilient against the encroaching despair, reminded him that the darkest paths often lead to the brightest dawns. With this fragile hope cradled in his heart, Eli stepped into the *Valley of Lamentation*, determined to wrestle his way toward the light.

The nights in the Valley were interminable, a relentless procession of solitary hours. The oppressive silence of his shattered abode was a constant companion, echoing the turmoil within Eli's soul. Visions of better days taunted him, fleeting and cruel. With each silent plea to the heavens, Eli's spirit battled the looming specter of despair.

Yet again, he implored, *"How long, O Lord? Will You hide Your face from me forever?"* His voice, laden with sorrow, filled the hollow emptiness around him. But the heavens held their peace, leaving Eli grappling with his fading faith and encroaching despair.

On the precipice of surrender, Eli's soul teetered. Still, a stubborn whisper of defiance within him spoke of hope and redemption. This whisper was a lifeline in the tempest, a call to endure the night. With every fiber of his being, Eli clung to this hope, a beacon in the consuming darkness.

One night, amid his most profound despondency, the essence of his grandmother's faith came to him like a balm. Her words from years past echoed in his heart: *"Even in the blackest nights, a glimmer of hope shines for those who dare to seek the light."* These words, imbued with her enduring spirit, fortified Eli, infusing him with the strength to rise from the ashes of his despair.

But as he embraced this newfound resolve, a chilling presence materialized from the shadows. A figure, sinister and foreboding, its eyes alight with malevolence, approached him. *"You cannot escape,"* it whispered venomously, manifesting his darkest fears. *"I am the weaver of your nightmares, the harbinger of your undoing."*

Eli recoiled in fear, his heart pounding with terror as he faced the embodiment of darkness that stood before him. The sinister presence seemed to be reaching out to claim him, to drag him into an abyss from which there might be no return. Eli's mind raced with fear and confusion as he struggled to find a way to resist the alluring pull of the darkness.

But then, something within him stirred. It was a memory of his grandmother's unwavering faith and the lessons she had imparted to him. With newfound clarity and determination, Eli realized that this was not just a battle for his spirit, but for his very soul. He knew he had to resist the darkness and fight with all his might, drawing on his inner strength and the teachings of his beloved grandmother.

This confrontation marked the beginning of a profound journey. As the malign figure loomed closer, intent on engulfing him in despair, Eli found a surge of defiance within himself. This moment, fraught with peril, was also filled with the promise of triumph. Eli knew he must endure and fight for the light that existed beyond the darkness. With a prayer whispered for strength, he prepared to face whatever lay ahead, knowing his journey through the *Valley of Lamentation* was only just beginning.

Chapter 2: The Hope of Redemption

In the aftermath of Hurricane Redemption, *Sotira City* was left in ruins, a desolate cityscape marred by the storm's fierce wrath. The once towering buildings, now reduced to rubble and debris, were a painful reminder of the devastation that had befallen the city. Their facades shattered, reflecting the brokenness of the city's soul, and the streets were littered with fallen trees, twisted steel, and scattered belongings. Eli, like many others, had lost everything in the storm. His life was uprooted, and his dreams were now scattered like the debris around him. As he navigated through the new labyrinth of loss and uncertainty, he couldn't help but wonder if there was still hope for the city's future.

As Eli walked aimlessly through the desolate streets, he stumbled upon a glimmer of hope - a humble shelter that had been constructed by the unwavering efforts of selfless volunteers. This sanctuary was a tapestry of human endurance and perseverance that drew Eli towards it with an irresistible force, like the moon's pull on the rising tide. Amidst the sea of displaced faces, Eli saw a faint but unyielding light of hope that shone through the despair and chaos. The eyes of the people he encountered bore witness to the horrors they had endured, yet they remained steadfast in their resolve to overcome the darkness of their present circumstances.

Eli found himself walking through a dimly lit and eerie space, his eyes struggling to adjust to the darkness. The only sound he could hear was the soft rustling of his clothes as he moved forward. Suddenly, a gentle yet potent glow eliminated the shadows in front of him, illuminating the path ahead. As he drew closer, he could see that the glow was emanating from a figure standing in front of him. It was Jeremiah, his friend and mentor.

The darkness was all-encompassing, the blackness so thick that it seemed to swallow up everything around them. But amidst this oppressive gloom, Jeremiah's presence shone like a beacon of hope. His aura was gentle and delicate yet possessed a potent power that repelled the shadows and kept them at bay. Eli felt an immense sense of relief upon seeing his mentor's glow. It was a reassurance that he was not alone in this eerie and foreboding space.

Jeremiah's light was more than just a mere illumination. It was a source of comfort and safety that enveloped Eli, shielding him from the unknown dangers that lurked in the darkness. As he moved forward, Jeremiah's glow made the path ahead clearer and less daunting. Eli's eyes struggled at first to adjust to the dim light, but with time, they adapted, and the surroundings became more visible.

Jeremiah warmly welcomed Eli with a gentle yet powerful affirmation, *"Welcome, my son.*

Even in the darkest of hours, the brightest stars can be born. Hold tight to your faith, and it will not falter, no matter how much it is tested."

In the midst of the eerie silence, and amplified movements, Jeremiah's presence was a constant source of guidance and protection for Eli. Eli knew that as long as he was under his mentor's wise and watchful eye, he could confidently navigate through the space.

Eli was moved by the honesty in Jeremiah's words, and the way he radiated a sense of tranquility and strength. As they stood together in the dimly lit area, Eli felt a renewed sense of optimism and resolve. He was reminded that even in the most trying of times, there is always a flicker of light to be found, and that his faith would guide him through the darkness.

As Eli listened to Jeremiah's impassioned divine utterances, his mind was completely consumed by the words which took root in his troubled heart. For the first time in a long while, he felt a glimmer of hope. Despite the overwhelming challenges facing their city, Jeremiah's unyielding determination and unwavering faith inspired Eli to join him in his noble quest to mend the shattered spirit of their community.

Together, they set out on an arduous journey to knit together the tattered fabric of their community, offering solace and comfort to those who had lost their way. As they worked tirelessly, their efforts slowly but surely began to bear fruit, as more and more people were touched by their kindness and compassion. Despite the many obstacles they faced, Eli and Jeremiah remained steadfast in their mission, knowing that every small act of kindness could make a difference in the lives of those around them.

The first challenge that they faced was nothing short of monumental. They were tasked with the daunting responsibility of restoring a sense of community spirit in a place that had been deeply entrenched in despair. As they navigated through the neighborhoods that had been ravaged by the storm, they were confronted with heart-wrenching stories of loss. But amidst the devastation, they also stumbled upon inspiring tales of heroism. They heard about families who had selflessly shielded one another from the storm's fury, and strangers who had become beacons of hope for those in peril. With every story they encountered, the thread of resilience was woven a little tighter into the fabric of *Sotira City*.

As the seeds of hope were sown, a few hearts remained closed to them. A powerful orator named *Heh-lel* had convinced many to embrace skepticism and pessimism instead. He argued that redemption was just an illusion, and that the world was too full of pain to ever be truly healed. Despite the efforts of the hopeful, his message continued to spread like wildfire, leaving many feeling lost and helpless.

As Eli and Jeremiah began to lay the foundation of their fledgling efforts, they were met with a new challenge. The followers of *Heh-lel*, once loyal to the cause, had grown disillusioned and fearful. Their words, like venom, threatened to cast a dark shadow over the fragile shoots of hope that Eli had started to nurture. It was a daunting task, but Eli and Jeremiah knew that they could not let these naysayers bring them down. They would have to find a way to rise above the negativity and push forward with their mission.

At a crucial juncture, Eli found himself in a difficult situation with no way out. However, to his surprise, he found an unlikely support in *Sarah*[5], a woman who appeared to have an unshakable faith. Despite having faced numerous setbacks in her life, Sarah's unwavering faith in the divine had made her an epitome of resilience and strength for those around her. Eli was moved by her resolute spirit and was inspired to confront *Heh-lel's* false narrative head-on, thanks to Sarah's unwavering support.

Eli brought the community together and shared his own journey of doubt and renewal. He emphasized that in our darkest moments, it is not a sign of absence but a call to deeper faith. His words resonated with everyone present, as he spoke of the divine tapestry being woven in their lives. Each thread of sorrow and joy creates a richer, more beautiful whole. This realization helped everyone to see that they are part of something bigger, something divine.

As the first rays of the sun began to illuminate the once-bewildered streets of *Sotira City*, a renewed sense of hope and purpose began to fill the air. The sounds of physical labor that had once echoed throughout the city had now been replaced by the softer, deeper sounds of heartfelt conversations and communal prayer that resonated through the air.

Eli, Jeremiah, and Sarah were three wise Oracles who had taken upon themselves to bring hope and healing to the people of *Sotira City*. Their efforts were not confined to just rebuilding the damaged structures of the city, but their focus was on something much deeper. They were dedicated to mending the emotional wounds of the community, who had gone through a traumatic experience of losing their homes, loved ones, and their sense of security.

With their profound wisdom, discernment, and compassion, the three Oracles worked sacrificially to uplift the spirits of the people and point them to *The Light*. They listened patiently to their stories of pain and loss and offered them words of comfort and encouragement. They organized healing sessions and workshops, where people could come together and share their experiences and find solace in each other's company.

The Oracles' efforts did not go unnoticed. Slowly but surely, the people of *Sotira City* began to heal. They found the strength to rebuild their lives and their community, all thanks to the tireless efforts of the three selfless *Oracles of The Most High.*

With each passing day, their efforts began to bear fruit as broken spirits started to heal, and a sense of community was reignited among the people. In homes, parks, and makeshift gathering spots, individuals shared their stories of loss and resilience, weaving together a tapestry of shared faith and experiences that brought them closer together.

Despite the prevalent chaos and destruction that still loomed over the city, a strong sense of hope began to emerge among its residents. This hope was not rooted in the physical reconstruction of the buildings, but rather in the emotional and spiritual renewal of the people. Eli, Jeremiah, and Sarah's unwavering commitment to the city and their efforts to support the community brought the residents together, creating bonds that were stronger than the structures they once occupied. The inspiring actions of these individuals instilled hope and motivated the community to work towards a brighter future.

Through collective reflection, empathy, and a renewed focus on spiritual growth, the people of *Sotira City* crafted a future that was brighter, not just in appearance but in essence. This new dawn was marked by the quiet strength of a community united in hope and healed in spirit, rather than the noise of construction.

Despite the visible signs of progress in the city's recovery, the pernicious influence of *Heh-lel* continued to pose a serious challenge. He had not given up but instead resorted to more insidious tactics, spreading uncertainty and disunity with a surgical precision. Eli came to a realization that the battle for the city's identity was not confined to the physical realm but extended to the intangible realm of its people's thoughts and emotions. The stakes of this conflict were high, and the outcome would determine the fate of the city's soul.

Eli was deeply troubled by the insidious spread of *Heh-lel's* poisonous words, which was sowing seeds of despair and hopelessness among the people. Determined to counteract this growing threat, Eli came up with a bold plan. He organized a series of gatherings where people shared tales of hope, resilience, and divine interventions. These stories, which were powerful testimonials of faith, acted as powerful antidotes to the venomous influence of *Heh-lel*. Through Eli's efforts, the people were able to find the strength to resist the negativity and despair, and embrace a more positive and hopeful outlook on life.

In the midst of all the stories, Eli shared a moment of clarity that left us all in awe. He envisioned a city that wasn't just reconstructed, but reborn; a community that wasn't defined by its location, but its purpose. *"We hold the power to shape our future, we aren't slaves to our past,"* Eli's words echoed through the room like a beacon of hope, drowning out any doubts we had.

As the community united and rallied around this new vision of hope and progress, the once-powerful influence of *Heh-lel* began to slowly diminish. However, Eli knew that the battle was far from over. The seeds of discord that had been sown by *Heh-lel* were deep and dark, capable of sprouting anew if left unchallenged.

But Eli was not alone in his quest for a better future. He was fortified by his companions, armed with faith, and ready to face any challenge that lay ahead. The path before them was long and winding, filled with trials and obstacles that would test their resolve at every turn. Yet, Eli remained steadfast in his commitment to the cause.

Step by step, Eli and his companions were rewriting the story of *Sotira City,* one that promised to bring hope and redemption to the city and its people. Their journey was not an easy one, but their perseverance and unwavering determination brought them closer to their vision of a brighter future with each passing day.

As the chapter of reconstruction unfolded, Eli's dream of a redeemed community became more tangible, a testament to the enduring power of hope and faith. But while the city slowly healed, *Heh-lel's* shadowy figure lurked in the darkness plotting his next move. Though the storm of his making had passed, the winds of conflict were still to come, threatening to shatter the fragile peace and hope that Eli and his companions had fought so hard to achieve.

Chapter 3: The Temptation of Envy

As Eli and Jeremiah meandered through the convoluted streets of *Sotira City's* bustling downtown district, they couldn't help but sense an overwhelming feeling of ambition and desire that seemed to fill the air like a thick fog. It was as if the towering skyscrapers and bustling crowds were all in competition with one another - trying to outdo each other in terms of power, wealth and influence.

At the center of this swirling vortex of greed and envy stood the formidable *Prospera Corp*—a mammoth conglomerate led by the mysterious and enigmatic *Marcus Prospera*. His wealth and influence were like magnets that drew in who craved his power and prestige, leaving them hopelessly ensnared in his web of influence. It was a storm that threatened to swallow up anyone who dared to succumb to its seductive allure.

As Eli gazed upon Marcus Prospera striding through the bustling streets, he was struck by the commanding presence he exuded. People around him looked on with a mix of admiration and reverence, drawn to his success and the aura of prosperity that surrounded him. Despite this, Eli couldn't shake off a sense of unease. He felt that something was lurking beneath the surface - a darkness that threatened to swallow those who dared to aspire to Marcus's accomplishments.

Eli was both fascinated and concerned by Marcus's allure. He couldn't help but be tempted by the promise of wealth and power that seemed to come with the territory. But as he drew closer to Marcus and his company, he felt an ever-increasing sense of foreboding. The glittering mirage that had once seemed so alluring now appeared to be a trap, with the true cost of

Prospera Corp's success becoming ever more apparent.

Eli felt the weight of his conscience bearing down upon him, reminding him that the true cost of success was often more than what met the eye. Despite the temptations, he knew that he needed to stay true to his values and not be drawn into the darkness that seemed to lurk beneath the surface.

In that moment of temptation, Jeremiah appeared beside him, his voice a calm and steady presence amidst the chaotic city. *"Be careful my son,"* he warned, reminding him of the dangers that lurked in the shadows. *"The pursuit of material possessions leads only to emptiness and despair. True wealth lies not in what you have but in the richness of your soul."*

As the words echoed in Eli's mind, he felt a surge of determination to follow the path of righteousness and integrity. He knew that true wealth could never be measured by material possessions, but by the purity of one's heart and the depth of one's character. Eli continued his journey, finding comfort in his faith and the knowledge that true wealth could not be bought or sold. He believed that it was only found in the embrace of a loving *Yahweh* who held the keys to both heaven and earth.

Eli remained vigilant against the potential temptations that lay on his path, knowing that the true test of his faith was yet to come. However, he had no idea that a new adversary was lurking in the shadows, waiting for the right moment to strike. This malevolent force was determined to undermine his resolve and tarnish his reputation in the eyes of the world. Eli's heart was heavy with the weight of the unknown adversary, but he was determined to stay on the path of righteousness and integrity.

Little did Eli know, as he bravely held his ground against the seductive temptations of

Prospera Corp, a dark and malicious force was already at work, lurking in the shadows and plotting his downfall through a web of cunning deceit and manipulation. This sinister entity was none other than the mastermind of evil *Heh-lel*, who had already ensnared *Sotira City* in his wicked schemes. *Heh-lel* had devised a plan to shatter Eli's reputation and sow discord among those who followed the path of light, and to carry out this nefarious plan, he had enlisted the help of his most wicked and cunning minion - the demon ***Jezebel***[9], whose unmatched malevolence and deceit made her the perfect tool for *Heh-lel's* twisted machinations.

Jezebel was a master manipulator who possessed a remarkable ability to sway those around her with her charming demeanor and persuasive language. She was a force to be reckoned with, executing her plan with precision and leaving no stone unturned. Her primary objective was to discredit and destroy Eli, a respected prophet of the Most High. Jezebel achieved this by weaving a complex web of lies, half-truths, and insinuations, raising suspicion and doubt in everyone she poisoned. She whispered slanderous accusations to Eli's family, friends, and followers, causing them to question and lose faith in him and his teachings. Jezebel was cunning and strategic, carefully calculating her actions to undermine Eli's authority and diminish his influence. Her nefarious plan ultimately succeeded, leaving Eli isolated and vulnerable to her attacks.

Amidst the tumultuous and fiery controversy that engulfed him, Eli found himself besieged and surrounded by former allies who had suddenly turned against him in a frenzy of fear and mistrust. It seemed as though the very foundation of his faith was being pierced by a barrage of accusations that flew at him like arrows. As the storm raged on with increasing ferocity, the flames of hope within him threatened to extinguish.

However, Eli remained steadfast in his convictions and refused to be swayed by the tide of lies and deceit. He stood firm alongside his loyal friend Jeremiah, determined to face his accusers with unwavering courage and integrity. For he knew that the truth would ultimately prevail over the darkness that sought to consume them. And so, with unwavering persistence, he braced himself for the battle ahead, ready to emerge victorious against all odds.

As the allegations piled up against Eli, he felt an intense pressure that he had never experienced before. His confidence was shaken, and he was on the verge of losing all hope. However, he refused to let go of the possibility of redemption and the unwavering affection of the One who had granted him his mission. Despite the overwhelming challenges, he continued to hold on to his faith and his belief in a better tomorrow.

In spite of his unwavering determination, the tightly-knit community of *Sotira City* gradually disintegrated under the pernicious influence of Jezebel's insidious whispers. Her words infected their hearts and minds, corroding their faith in each other and causing them to turn on one another. What was once a harmonious and trusting community was now reduced to a shattered and fractured shell, where even the closest of friends and siblings were consumed by the treacherous web of deceit and manipulation.

Eli stood there, watching in despair, as the once-strong bonds that had held them together disintegrated before his very eyes. Doubt crept in, and he felt the weight of it pressing down on him. His mind was consumed with the question of whether he was truly worthy of the mantle of prophet or if he was nothing more than a fraud, as Jezebel had suggested.

Despite the chaos and confusion that surrounded him, Jeremiah remained a beacon of unwavering strength and wisdom. He guided Eli through the storm with his steadfast faith, and together, they stood firm as pillars of truth and integrity in a world that was consumed by lies and deceit. Their unwavering commitment to the truth made them a shining light in the darkness and an inspiration to all who really knew them.

Amid the storm's fury, Eli remained steadfast in his faith, convinced that the path of righteousness is not always easy, but it is always worth fighting for. He held on to hope, knowing that even in the face of betrayal and deceit, redemption was possible - not just for himself, but for his city and all those who choose to believe in the transformative power of truth and love, even in the darkest of nights.

During moments of uncertainty and hopelessness, Eli found comfort in prayer. He sought guidance and strength from the One who had called him to his purpose. Although the future remained unclear, he knew that as long as he remained faithful to the truth, he would come out of the storm stronger and more determined than ever before.

Eli was desperately holding onto hope of redemption, but he had a feeling that the worst was yet to come. In the shadows, *Heh-lel* watched with a sinister grin as his nefarious plan unfolded. He was fully aware that the true battle for Eli's soul had just begun. The darkness deepened with each passing moment, threatening to engulf them all in its all-consuming embrace. It was like a ravenous beast waiting to devour its prey.

The situation at *Sotira City* was becoming increasingly ominous. Eli was struggling to maintain the trust and support of those closest to him, as a cloud of doubt and suspicion hung over the community. He felt the weight of their accusatory stares and hushed murmurs, each one a sharp blade cutting into his already exhausted soul, threatening to shatter his resolve. The atmosphere was tense and overwhelming, and Eli was caught in the middle of a fierce battle for his reputation and relationships.

Despite the ceaseless chaos that surrounded them, a small flame of optimism persisted in the abyss - a signal of hope that refused to yield to the tempest. This enduring spark was fueled by the steadfast devotion of a handful of close companions and supporters who stood resolutely beside Eli, unyielding in their belief in his honor and virtue even as they weathered the relentless barrage of deceit and defamation that beset them.

Eli's journey was not an easy one, but he was fortunate to have Sarah[5] by his side. She was a remarkable woman, with an unshakeable belief in the power of faith and an unwavering loyalty to Eli and his cause. Even in the face of the most daunting challenges, Sarah remained a constant source of strength and courage for Eli, providing him with the unwavering support he needed to carry on. Together, they worked tirelessly to combat the insidious accusations of Jezebel, using the power of truth and love to overcome the negativity and hatred that threatened to undermine their efforts. Despite the obstacles they faced, Eli and Sarah never lost sight of their goals, and their partnership remained a shining example of what can be achieved through perseverance, determination, and unwavering faith.

Their noble quest was to extend a hand of empathy and understanding to those who had fallen prey to Jezebel's deceitful ways. Despite facing countless obstacles and hostility from their adversaries, their resolve never wavered. They firmly believed that the unyielding light of truth would eventually penetrate the veil of darkness and steer them towards the path of righteousness.

Their persistent determination and unyielding spirit paid off in the end, as they successfully completed their mission with great success. Their resolute faith, unwavering loyalty, and limitless love had a profound impact on the lives of the people they met, leaving an unforgettable impression on their hearts and souls. Their story serves as a powerful reminder of the strength and resilience of the human spirit in the face of challenges.

Eli and his allies were determined to take back their city from the clutches of deception. But as they battled to restore order, a sinister figure watched from the shadows with a twisted smile. *Heh-lel* was up to something again, and his malevolent intent was palpable. He knew that as long as the people were plagued by doubt and discord, *Sotira City* would remain vulnerable to his wicked influence. It was a dangerous game of manipulation and deceit, and *Heh-lel* was determined to win at any cost.

As the war for the heart of *Sotira City* waged on, Eli and his companions braced themselves for the ultimate clash—a decisive face-off between the forces of veracity and deception, illumination and obscurity, which would decide the future of their metropolis and the course of their spirits.

In the final showdown, only one person could claim victory. The fate of all that was good rested on the shoulders of those who were brave enough to trust in the power of redemption and the resilience of hope. For in that moment, the choice between light and darkness was theirs to make, and the world waited with bated breath for their decision.

The conflict between truth and deception had been on the rise for an extended period, and now *Sotira City* found themselves at a critical juncture. They had to make a momentous decision - whether to give in to the darkness that threatened to engulf them or rise up and embrace the light of redemption and forgiveness.

At the forefront of this spiritual battleground stood Eli, a man who was weary yet resolute. His heart was heavy with the weight of the burden he bore, but even in his darkest hour, he clung to the hope that his city would make the right decision. He hoped they would choose the path of righteousness and integrity, rejecting the lies and deceit that had threatened to tear them apart.

Eli was a man of great faith and resilience who had always been a respected leader among his people. However, as the accusations against him grew louder and more vehement, he began to doubt his own abilities. The constant barrage of hatred and mistrust from all sides began to chip away at his core, and in moments of vulnerability, he found himself questioning his own worthiness to lead.

He wondered if the price of redemption was too high and whether he could ever regain the trust of those who had once looked up to him. He felt helpless and lost, unsure of what to do next. But then, Jeremiah appeared at Eli's side, just when he needed support the most.

Jeremiah's unwavering faith and resolve gave Eli hope and illuminated the path forward. With Jeremiah's guidance, Eli was able to find the courage to face his accusers and defend himself against their baseless accusations. Jeremiah reminded Eli of the power of forgiveness and how it could mend even the most broken of relationships.

With Jeremiah by his side, Eli was able to confront his doubts and fears head-on. He felt brave and ready to face any challenge that lay ahead, knowing that he would emerge from the situation stronger and more resilient than ever before. Thanks to Jeremiah's unwavering support and guidance, Eli was able to weather the storm and emerge victorious.

With the understanding that forgiveness was the key to unshackling their city from the chains of bondage that held it captive, Eli and his allies embarked on a quest to confront the darkness that loomed over them. They knew that the only way to break free from the grip of hatred that threatened to consume them was to extend a hand of grace and compassion to those who accused them. With hearts open to the possibility of reconciliation and redemption, they offered their adversaries the opportunity to renounce their weapons of animosity and embrace the transformative power of forgiveness.

As they set out on their journey, the shadowy figure of *Heh-lel* lurked in the background, observing their every move with malevolent intent. His wicked laughter reverberated through the darkness, as he anticipated the failure of Eli and his allies. *Heh-lel* knew that as long as the seeds of discord remained planted in the hearts of the people, the city would remain vulnerable to his influence, and he would continue to manipulate and deceive, making it a pawn in his evil game.

As the battle for the very essence of *Sotira City* continued to escalate, Eli and his supporters braced themselves for the ultimate clash - a confrontation that would determine the destiny of their city and the course of their souls. The conflict pitted truth against lies, light against darkness, and the stakes were impossibly high.

Eli and his allies knew that the outcome of the battle was critical, as only one side could ultimately emerge victorious. The weighty choice between good and evil rested in the hands of those who had the courage to believe in the power of redemption and the ultimate triumph of hope over despair. The fate of their city and the destiny of their souls hung in the balance, and the tension was palpable as they prepared to face their ultimate challenge.

Amidst the ruins of their once-beautiful city, Eli and his companions stood tall and resolute. Their hearts were heavy, but they refused to be defeated. The echoes of conflict faded into the distance, and as the dust settled, they felt a glimmer of hope for a brighter tomorrow. The journey towards healing and clemency was just beginning, and it would lead them to *The Power and Healing of Forgiveness*. There, they would discover the true strength of redemption, and the courage to rise above the rubble and build a new, more resilient community.

Eli was filled with curiosity and uncertainty about what lay ahead for him. He had been praying for a specific outcome, but he couldn't help but wonder if his prayers would be answered. He hoped that the path ahead would bring him the healing and forgiveness he so desperately needed, but he also knew that there were many challenges and obstacles he would have to overcome to achieve his goal. Despite the uncertainty, Eli remained hopeful and determined, ready to face whatever lay ahead with courage and resilience.

Chapter 4: The Healing of Forgiveness

In the wake of his encounter with the allure of wealth and power, Eli found himself grappling with a new challenge—one that tested the very essence of his character and faith. As he journeyed alongside Jeremiah through the streets of *Sotira City,* they came upon a neighborhood ravaged not by physical destruction, but by the scars of broken relationships and fractured souls.

In the midst of the serene suburban neighborhoods, there existed a community that was plagued by animosity and hostility. The once-affable relationships between families had deteriorated into bitter feuds, and friendships that were once cherished had faltered beyond repair. The hearts of the residents had hardened against each other, each person harboring emotional wounds that were too profound to be easily mended.

Eli and Jeremiah embarked on a heartfelt journey, driven by their deep compassion for those who were suffering. They were determined to bring healing and comfort to those who were broken-hearted, guided by the beacon of forgiveness and the promise of redemption. They took each step with care and purpose, with the intention of repairing the damage done and restoring the bonds that had been severed. Their words were filled with the power of reconciliation, and their actions were fueled by the purest form of love. They knew that mending what had been torn asunder would not be easy, but they remained steadfast in their mission, working determinedly to repair one shattered relationship at a time.

Their journey had been long and arduous, fraught with obstacles at every turn. As they approached the modest home of the Johnson family, once known for their tight-knit bond, Eli felt a sense of trepidation gnawing at his resolve. Years of misunderstanding and mistrust had left deep emotional scars, and the weight of their pain threatened to overwhelm him.

As Eli attentively listened to the conflicting accounts of the parties involved, he couldn't help but feel a deep sense of sorrow engulfing him. He was well aware that Jezebel was behind this, causing the pain and hurt that were almost tangible. He knew that the journey towards healing the wounds would not be an easy one. However, even amidst the tears and allegations, he could sense a tiny glimmer of hope flickering to life. It was like a ray of light shining through the darkness of despair, giving him the strength to persevere.

Eli, accompanied by Jeremiah, extended a hand of forgiveness to the Johnson family. He offered them the opportunity to release their past grievances and embrace the liberating power of forgiveness. This small yet powerful act of kindness and compassion had the potential to heal even the deepest wounds and inspire a brighter future.

As the presence of forgiveness entered the atmosphere, the barriers that had once stood between people, dividing them from one another, began to crumble and fall. In their place, a sense of unity and mutual understanding emerged, ushering in a newfound era of peace and harmony. Forgiveness flowed like a soothing balm, healing the wounds of the past. Eli watched in wonder as miraculous transformations began to take place. Broken hearts were made whole again, fractured relationships were restored, and souls that had been held captive by the chains of unforgiveness were finally set free.

As the sun sank beneath the horizon, painting the sky in brilliant shades of amber and crimson, Eli felt a profound sense of peace settle over

Sotira City. It was a peace that came not from the influence of wealth or power, but from the transformative power of forgiveness and grace. Eli knew that their journey was far from over, but he found comfort in the knowledge that with each act of forgiveness, they drew one step closer to the ultimate redemption that awaited them all.

As Eli stood there, looking out at the vast expanse of land before him, he felt a sense of peace wash over him. It was as if all of the worries and fears that had plagued him before had suddenly been lifted, and he was left with a feeling of calm and stillness.

And then something miraculous happened. It was like a jar of oil was poured over his head, a warm and soothing sensation that spread throughout his body, filling him with a renewed sense of hope and purpose.

In that moment, Eli felt as if he had been transformed from the inside out. The wounds of his past, the hurts and regrets that had held him back for so long, were suddenly gone. And in their place, he felt a new sense of possibility and potential, a belief that anything was possible if he only had the courage to try.

As he stood there, taking in the beauty of the world around him, Eli knew that a new era had begun. One filled with hope, joy, and the promise of a brighter future.

Eli and Jeremiah had decided to bring reconciliation to families who were in need. During their mission, they met the Rodriguez family who had been involved in a bitter family feud that had lasted for years. Misunderstandings and old grievances had fueled the feud, which had been festering like wounds left unattended.

As Eli approached the doorstep of the Rodriguez family, he felt the weight of the task ahead. He knew that resolving years of animosity would require more than mere words. It would require a touch of grace that only *Yahweh* could provide. He took a deep breath and knocked on the door, hoping for a positive response.

When the door opened, Eli could see the tension and mistrust on the faces of the family members. However, he was undeterred and began to speak with them, listening patiently to their stories, and trying to understand the root cause of their conflicts. He knew that this would be a long and challenging process, but he was determined to persevere.

Eli and Jeremiah were dedicated to repairing the broken relationships among the Rodriguez family members. They invested extensive efforts in fostering a sense of unity, urging them to release their resentments and strive for reconciliation. In order to accomplish this, they skillfully guided the family members through a structured process of healing. They provided the family with the tools and techniques necessary to communicate more effectively and empathetically, encouraging them to gain a deeper understanding of each other's experiences. Their compassionate and diligent efforts ultimately resulted in the restoration of harmony and peace among the Rodriguez family.

The Rodriguez family was able to overcome their differences and find a way to move forward together. Eli and Jeremiah felt delighted to see that their efforts had paid off, and they knew that they had played a small role in bringing healing and restoration to this troubled family.

Eli drew upon the profound power of the prophetic word, as he began to speak words of truth and love that seemed to resonate deep within the hearts of those who listened. His voice was strong and clear, ringing out like a clarion call in the stillness of the night, piercing through the oppressive weight of discord that had been suffocating the atmosphere. With each proclamation, he felt the atmosphere shift, the air around him becoming charged with a sense of peace and tranquility. His words were like a balm to those who had been struggling, offering hope in the midst of uncertainty, and a sense of direction in times of confusion. As he continued to speak, the power of his words seemed to grow stronger, and the impact of his message more profound.

Eli felt a wave of relief wash over him as he spoke the words of forgiveness, hoping against hope that they would have the desired effect. As he looked up at the faces of the Rodriguez family, he saw a mixture of surprise and euphoria. For years, walls had stood between them, built up by hurt and resentment that had festered for too long. But now, as the words left his lips, he watched in awe as those walls crumbled and fell away before his very eyes. The tension that had once hung heavily in the air dissipated, replaced by a newfound sense of unity and understanding. Eli felt a sense of peace settle over him as he realized that his words of forgiveness had brought healing to a family that had been torn apart for far too long.

As the family gathered together, embracing one another, tears streamed down their faces - a mix of both joy and sorrow. It was a moment of release, a time to let go of the past and embrace the hope of a brighter future. And in that moment, something truly remarkable happened - it was as if a wave of healing forgiveness washed over the entire neighborhood, like sweet rain.

Eli watched in awe as he realized that the power of forgiveness had once again triumphed over the forces of darkness. It was a moment of transformation, a time when the impossible became possible. And as the family basked in the warmth of this newfound forgiveness, Eli knew that this was a moment that would stay with them forever. For in that moment, the path to redemption had been illuminated for all who dared to walk in its light.

Eli's reputation for performing miraculous acts began to spread like wildfire throughout *Sotira City*. As acts of healing the sick, comforting the grieving, and performing other seemingly impossible feats filled the air and reached the ears of every resident in the town, people began to believe that he held the key to their hopes and dreams and a sense of excitement and anticipation began to take hold in their hearts.

As the stories of these miracles continued to circulate, more and more people flocked to see him, from all corners of the town. They came in droves, hoping to witness the Truth of his powers with their own eyes. And as they saw him in action, they couldn't help but feel a sense of awe and wonder.

The people of *Sotira City* were astonished by Eli's visit. They had never experienced such a profound feeling of love before. His mere presence brought a glimmer of hope to their lives, and the more they saw of him, the more they began to believe that he was indeed a miracle worker.

Over time, despite early skepticism from some, Eli's reputation as an honest and prophetic man continued to grow. People from all walks of life reported experiencing the miraculous touch of the Divine, which seemed to alleviate their pain and suffering. People of all ages and backgrounds were drawn to him, each with their own unique story of affliction, hoping that the healing power of forgiveness could bring them relief.

As people started to hear more and more about the incredible encounters with Eli and those who followed him, a feeling of positivity and rejuvenation began to take hold in the hearts of those who had previously been struggling with feelings of despair and isolation. The presence that was upon Eli transformed these individuals, filling them with a renewed sense of hope and purpose. Many saw him as a symbol of light in a world that often seemed dark and uncertain, and they held onto this beacon of hope as they navigated the challenges of their daily lives. Through his actions, many people could find the strength and resilience they needed to face their difficulties with courage and determination.

Eli was known for his wisdom and compassion, and it was no surprise that many people sought his guidance. Among those who came to him seeking help was a young woman named *Uriel*[6].

Uriel had been carrying the weight of guilt and shame for years. She had made mistakes in the past and had convinced herself that she was unworthy of love and forgiveness. The burden had become too heavy to bear, and she needed someone to help her release it.

As she listened to Eli's words of grace and compassion, something stirred within her spirit. A glimmer of hope that had long lay dormant began to awaken. Eli's kindness and understanding made her feel safe enough to share her secrets, and she poured out her heart to him, tears streaming down her face.

Uriel sat across from Eli and opened up about the secrets that had tormented her for years. She spoke of the mistakes she had made, the people she had hurt, and the pain she had caused herself. But instead of judgment, Eli listened with an open heart, offering her *The Healing of Forgiveness* she so desperately needed.

As Eli guided her through her struggles, Uriel found the strength to let go of her past and embrace a new future. With each passing moment, she felt the weight of her burdens lifting, replaced by a sense of peace and freedom that she had never known before. It was as if a new reality had opened up before her, one in which she was no longer bound by her past or her pain.

As she listened to Eli's kind and compassionate words, the darkness that had wrapped itself around her soul began to recede, like a fog lifting to reveal a bright, clear day.

Eli's voice echoed through the room, filling it with a sense of authority that commanded attention. As his words flowed, they seemed to carry a weight and power that transcended mere speech. It was as if each syllable was imbued with the divine, carrying with it the force of the prophetic word.

With each proclamation, Eli seemed to be speaking directly to her heart, unlocking the deepest parts of her being and releasing her from the chains that had held her captive. And as she embraced him, tears streaming down her face, she knew that her life would never be the same again. For in that moment, she had been touched by something truly divine, a love and forgiveness that was beyond anything she had ever experienced before.

For in the presence of Eli, she had encountered *The Power of Redemption*—a power that could heal even the deepest wounds and restore what had been lost. And as she walked away from their encounter, her heart lighter than it had been in years, she knew that she had been given a second chance at life—a chance to live in the fullness of *Yahweh's* grace and mercy.

Uriel left their meeting feeling lighter and more hopeful than she had in years, grateful for the wisdom and understanding of her mentor. The experience had taught her *The Power of Forgiveness* and the importance of embracing a brighter future.

As Eli's repute and influence continued to spread throughout *Sotira City*, the malevolent force, *Heh-lel*, who was responsible for the prevailing chaos and despair, grew increasingly concerned about the impact that Eli's message of hope and redemption might have on the people. Determined to put an end to Eli's message once and for all, *Heh-lel* devised a devious plan to undermine Eli's credibility once again.

The powerful demonic entity *Heh-lel*, once again devised a plan to hinder the message of hope and redemption being preached by Eli in Sotira City. To execute his plan, *Heh-lel* summoned his most cunning and manipulative demon, *Jezebel*, to the city once again. *Jezebel* was known for her ability to manipulate people's minds and turn them against each other. Her ultimate goal was to discredit Eli's message and make people question its validity.

Jezebel worked tirelessly to cause confusion and chaos in the city. She used her lies to create mistrust and suspicion among the people, and to turn them against each other. Her successful tactics involved attacking the weak and weary, questioning their beliefs, causing many to doubt Eli's message of hope and redemption.

Jezebel's tactics were subtle and insidious. She whispered lies and false promises into the ears of the people, twisting the truth and distorting reality until nothing was as it seemed. Under her influence, suspicion and mistrust flourished, poisoning the hearts of those who had once stood united in their quest for redemption.

Despite *Jezebel's* efforts, however, Eli continued to preach his message of hope and redemption. He reminded the people of the importance of unity and love, and encouraged them to resist *Jezebel's* attempts to sow discord. Eventually, the people of *Sotira City* saw through *Jezebel's* lies and were able to come together and support Eli's message once again.

Despite the challenges he faced, Eli remained steadfast in his commitment to his message of hope and forgiveness. He continued to stand before the crowds, proclaiming the message that had been entrusted to him, but he could feel the weight of *Jezebel's* influence pressing down upon him. Accusations were hurled, slanderous rumors spread like wildfire, attempting to shake the very foundation of his faith to its core once again. However, Eli remained resilient and determined, refusing to be swayed by the lies and deceit of *Heh-lel's* minions.

In the face of adversity, Eli remained steadfast and resolute. He stood firm in his unwavering faith and courage, trusting in the knowledge that he was not alone in this sacred task. Eli had an unshakable belief that *Yahweh, The One* who had called him, would never abandon him in his hour of need.

Despite the storms that raged around him, Eli continued to proclaim the message of redemption with a heart full of resolve. He was undeterred by the challenges that he faced, knowing that the battle was not his alone. Eli believed that the victory had already been won by *The One* who had conquered sin and death and held the keys to all creation.

As the darkness closed in around him, Eli lifted his voice in prayer, calling upon the name of the Lord to deliver him from the hands of his enemies. In that moment, he felt the presence of *Yahweh* descend upon him like a mighty rushing wind, filling him with a peace that surpassed all understanding. Eli knew that he was not alone and that he would be delivered from this difficult situation.

With renewed strength and determination, Eli faced his adversaries head-on, his eyes ablaze with the fire of divine purpose. For he knew that though the road ahead would be fraught with peril, he walked it not alone, but in the company of *The One* who had called him to this sacred mission—a mission of redemption, reconciliation, and ultimately, of victory.

The conflict between Eli, a brave and righteous leader, and the dark forces that threatened the peace and prosperity of his city had escalated to an unprecedented level. *Sotira City*, the epicenter of the battle, had become a battleground where Eli found himself facing a multitude of adversaries. These adversaries were determined to discredit his message, challenge his authority, and undermine his efforts to bring about positive change.

Amidst the ongoing conflict, chaos and destruction had taken over the city. The residents were faced with dangerous and life-threatening situations, putting their courage and resilience to the ultimate test. Despite the insurmountable odds, Eli remained determined to protect his people and uphold his values.

The battle for *Sotira City* had become a symbol of the struggle between good and evil, and Eli was at the forefront of this epic battle. He fought with all his might, drawing on his inner strength and the support of his allies. The outcome of this conflict would determine the fate of the city and its people, and Eli was determined to emerge victorious.

However, in the midst of the turmoil, Eli remained unshakable in his commitment to the truth. He drew strength from the knowledge that he was not alone in his fight. He knew that *Yahweh* who had chosen him for this sacred mission was by his side, guiding him every step of the way.

With the power of the prophetic word at his disposal and the assurance of divine protection, Eli forged ahead, his heart ablaze with the fire of righteousness. As he walked the treacherous path before him, he was aware of the dangers that lay ahead. But he was determined to stay the course, knowing that he was not fighting this battle alone. He trusted in the Lord to see him through to victory.

As Eli's unwavering faith and courage inspired the people of *Sotira City*, they began to rally around him, joining him in his quest for redemption. Together, they stood against the forces of darkness, united in prayer and worship, declaring victory in the name of the Lord. Their voices echoed through the city, a resounding testimony to the power of faith and the triumph of good over evil.

And as the city echoed with the sounds of worship and warfare, Eli knew that the tide was turning in their favor. For he had seen firsthand the power of *Yahweh* to overcome even the greatest of obstacles, and he knew that no weapon formed against them could stand against the might of the Almighty.

With each passing day, the darkness that had gripped *Sotira City* began to recede, replaced by the dawning light of a new day. And as Eli looked out upon the city, he saw signs of hope and renewal springing up like flowers in the desert, a testament to the faithfulness of *Yahweh* who never fails.

For in the end, it was not the strength of man nor the cunning of the enemy that determined the outcome of the battle, but the power of *Yahweh* working through willing hearts and surrendered lives. And as Eli stood amidst the ruins of the old, he knew that something beautiful was emerging—a city transformed by the power of redemption and grace, a beacon of hope in a world shrouded in darkness.

Eli stood in the midst of the rubble, gazing at the ruins of *Sotira City*, the city that had been the scene of a grueling spiritual battle. Despite the devastation that surrounded him, he felt a sense of peace and gratitude in his heart. The scars of the conflict were a testament to the power of truth, forgiveness, and reconciliation to overcome even the greatest of trials.

As the city began to rebuild and heal, Eli witnessed miracles unfolding before his very eyes. He saw broken relationships being restored, hearts being softened by the power of forgiveness, and souls being liberated from the chains of bitterness and resentment. In each moment of restoration, he saw the hand of *Yahweh* at work, guiding and shaping the destiny of His people according to His perfect will.

Eli marveled at the beauty of *Yahweh*'s handiwork, as he saw the city transform before his very eyes. The rebuilding process was slow, but the progress was evident. The scars were still visible, but the city was now alive with a newfound hope and resilience, which was a testament to the human spirit.

As the sun set over the horizon, casting a golden glow upon the city below, Eli lifted his voice in praise and thanksgiving to *The One* who had brought them through the storm. His words echoed through the streets of *Sotira City*, bringing a sense of peace that surpassed all understanding and filled the hearts of all who heard them.

Eli knew that the journey ahead would be long and fraught with challenges, but he was confident that they did not walk alone. For *The One* who had brought them this far would surely lead them safely home, guiding them with His light and sustaining them with His grace. And with this knowledge, Eli felt a sense of peace and hope that filled his heart and gave him the strength to face whatever lay ahead.

And so, as the stars twinkled overhead and the night enveloped the city in its embrace, Eli bowed his head in reverence and awe, humbled by the majesty of *The One* he served. For in that moment, he knew that they stood on the threshold of something truly miraculous—a future filled with hope, redemption, and the boundless love of their *Creator*.

Eli's eyes slowly closed as he let out a deep sigh, feeling a wave of gratitude wash over him. He knew that he had been through a lot, but in that moment, he felt an overwhelming sense of peace and comfort. As he whispered a prayer of thanks, he couldn't help but feel a renewed sense of hope and assurance. He knew that *Yahweh* who had brought him through the toughest of times would always be by his side, leading him towards a brighter tomorrow. With that thought, Eli felt a sense of calmness wash over him, filling him with a newfound strength to face whatever lay ahead.

Chapter 5: The Unity of Brotherhood

As Eli and Jeremiah continued their journey through the city of *Sotira City*, they couldn't help but be mesmerized by the diverse array of neighborhoods they encountered on the outskirts. Each neighborhood seemed to have its own unique character, yet they all coexisted amidst the sprawling landscape in perfect harmony. The streets were bustling with activity, as people of different cultures and backgrounds went about their daily lives.

As Eli and Jeremiah explored the vast expanse of land before them, they stumbled upon a tribe that was deeply divided by suspicion and fear. The unease was palpable in the air as they observed the tense atmosphere among the members of the tribe. The two travelers learned that the tribe had been plagued by a series of conflicts and mistrust, causing a rift between them that seemed impossible to bridge. Despite the vibrant tapestry of cultures and communities that surrounded them, this tribe seemed to be trapped in a never-ending cycle of mistrust and suspicion.

In the heart of this neighborhood stood a community center, a place where people from all walks of life gathered to seek refuge from the storms of life. Yet, despite their shared struggles and common humanity, the residents remained segregated by the invisible barriers of prejudice and misunderstanding. Eli and Jeremiah felt a sense of sadness as they saw how the community was divided, despite the fact that they shared the same space and resources.

With a determination to bridge the divide and unite the disparate factions, Eli and Jeremiah set out on a mission to bring people together. Their hearts were ablaze with a passion for unity and brotherhood. They knew that it would not be an easy task, but they were willing to do whatever it took to break down the walls that separated them. With words of reconciliation on their lips and acts of kindness in their hands, they sought to break down the barriers that separated them, one at a time. They believed that by showing kindness and compassion to each other, they could build a community that was stronger and more connected than ever before.

Eli and Jeremiah's journey took them to the simple home of the Hernandez family - a group of immigrants who had traveled a great distance to start anew in a foreign land. The family had encountered countless acts of discrimination and disrespect from their fellow citizens, which had made their existence a constant struggle. Eli bore witness to the Hernandez family's plight, and their hardships and struggles deeply moved him. He felt an intense urge to see justice and equality triumph over the hatred and bigotry that had plagued the world for far too long.

Encouraged by Jeremiah's unwavering support, Eli took a bold step toward healing the divisions within their community. He extended a heartfelt invitation to the community leaders, urging them to gather together in a spirit of unity and reconciliation. Eli was moved by an overwhelming sense of purpose, knowing he was being guided by *Yahweh* to share a message of hope and inspiration with this community. As they began to converse and share their thoughts and emotions, a palpable sense of camaraderie and *The Unity of Brotherhood* enveloped them like a warm blanket on a cold night. They were deeply touched by the power of their shared connection, and tears flowed freely as they felt their hearts open to one another.

As their conversation deepened, something prophetic began to happen. Walls that had once divided them started to crumble, and they found themselves united by a shared sense of purpose. They swapped stories about the obstacles they had faced and found that they had more in common than they had ever thought possible. Together, they prayed, brainstormed ideas, and hatched plans to create a warm, welcoming, and inclusive community. It was a beautiful moment that left them feeling empowered and inspired to make the world a better place, one step at a time.

Eli stood by his comrades, all of them working together towards a common goal. As they worked side by side, shoulder to shoulder, he was amazed at the miracles that unfolded before his very eyes. What was once a group of strangers had become friends, what were once enemies had become allies, and bonds of brotherhood had been forged in the fires of adversity.

As the sun gradually began to set, casting its golden rays upon the city below, Eli couldn't help but feel an overwhelming sense of peace wash over him. He felt as though he was witnessing something truly remarkable that he had never seen before in Sotira City. The community had finally achieved a level of unity that had eluded them for so long. This was not a unity that came from forcing everyone to be the same, but rather from embracing the differences and celebrating the diversity that existed within their community. It was a recognition that even though they had different backgrounds, cultures, and experiences, they were all human beings with the same faith, hopes, dreams, and aspirations. This newfound unity powered by their trust in Yahweh created a sense of belonging and acceptance that everyone could feel, and it was a beautiful thing to witness.

As he looked out at the beautiful city, Eli reflected on the journey that had brought them all there. It had been a difficult one, with many hardships along the way. But every act of kindness and compassion had brought them one step closer to their ultimate redemption. And even though there was still much work to be done, Eli took comfort in the knowledge that they were on the right path, and that they would get there together.

Eli and Jeremiah fearlessly poured out the love of *Yahweh* to everyone, transforming their community. Their message of unity and harmony inspired a newfound sense of purpose that galvanized the people, who banded together to stand tall and proud for their common cause. The buzz of excitement was palpable, a testament to the power of their efforts in bringing about positive change. The community was forever transformed, thanks to Eli and Jeremiah's unyielding commitment to spreading love and unity.

But as the winds of change swept through the town, a sinister force lurked in the shadows, plotting its next move. *Heh-lel*, the mastermind behind this malevolent scheme, seethed with anger at the sight of the community thriving. Determined to bring it down, he set his sights on infiltrating the very heart of the town and sowing the seeds of discord.

As the sun slowly began to set over the neighborhood, Eli's heart leapt at the sound of a rushing wind. It was an urgent message from a messenger of *Yahweh*, a source that Eli trusted above all others. The message contained troubling news of a clandestine meeting that was scheduled to take place at the edge of the city, in a realm that was accessible only to a select few. The meeting was to be attended by *Heh-lel's* agents, who were plotting their next move to wreak havoc in the city.

Eli knew that he had no time to waste. Without a moment's hesitation, he reached out to Jeremiah, his trusted mentor and spiritual advisor, for help. Together, they set out to uncover the truth and put an end to *Heh-lel's* sinister plans. *In the spirit*, they traversed the spiritual realm and arrived at the location of the meeting.

What they saw there was shocking. *Heh-lel's* agents had gathered in large numbers, and they were deep in discussion about their next move. Eli and Jeremiah listened intently, taking note of every detail. They knew that the fate of the city was at stake, and they were determined to ensure that justice prevailed.

With their covert mission accomplished, Eli and Jeremiah returned to the *physical realm*, their hearts heavy with the weight of the responsibility that had been placed upon them. But they knew that they had done what was necessary to expose the evil plans in order to protect the city from harm, and that gave them the strength to face whatever challenges lay ahead.

As they stepped out of Eli's house, they felt a cool breeze blowing, sending shivers down their spines. The night was dark, and the streets were deserted, with only the occasional stray dog barking in the distance. They moved swiftly and silently, their eyes darting around, scanning for any sign of danger.

As they advanced towards the outskirts of the bustling metropolis, they could discern the faint flicker of torches in the distance, casting an eerie glow on the otherwise dark and silent night. Hushed whispers and muffled voices drifted from *Heh-lel's* dimly lit chamber, where his minions were gathered.

As Eli and Jeremiah peered out from behind a massive boulder, the mysterious figures gathered in a tight circle. The darkness obscured their faces, but the intensity of their hushed whispers was unmistakable. The two protagonists listened intently, their hearts racing as they could here *Heh-lel' discuss* his sinister plans in the distance.

The air was thick with sulfur's smell as the minions plotted their clandestine operation. Each was acutely aware of the risk and danger involved if they were exposed to *The Light*.

Eli and Jeremiah moved closer with calculated precision, their every step was taken with utmost care to avoid detection and maintain their cover. Even the slightest mistake could spell disaster for their mission and shatter their hopes of success.

The palpable tension in the dark chamber was underscored by the eerie silence that permeated the space, punctuated only by the occasional hiss, growl, or shuffling of feet.

Eli and Jeremiah knew they had uncovered a dangerous plot that threaten *Sotira City's* peace. With a fierce determination burning in their hearts, they vowed to uncover the truth and end the vile machinations of *Heh-lel's* agents.

Eli and Jeremiah were *in the spirit,* as they listened as *Heh-lel's* emissaries laid out a plan to sow discord at the upcoming community festival—an event designed to celebrate the cultural diversity of *Sotira City.* The plan was cunning, involving spreading rumors and inciting rivalries among different cultural groups.

Eli had earlier received Revelation regarding an alarming plot threatening the safety of his community. He knew that the best course of action was to act proactively to protect his community from danger. Eli devised a plan to address the community, pre-empting the plot by being transparent about the details he had heard. He highlighted the importance of vigilance and unity in the face of such tactics.

On the day of the festival, Eli took the stage, his presence commanding and resolute. As he spoke of the threats lurking in the shadows, the community listened with rapt attention. His words instilled a sense of urgency, but also a sense of hope to the people. They felt empowered and strengthened by Eli's transparency and leadership.

Eli's counter-strategy of *Love and Light* exposed the darkness and turned the tables on *Heh-lel*, who had planned to use secrecy and deceit to carry out his plot. Eli exposed *Heh-lel's lies* and used his own weapons against him rendering his plans useless. By being transparent about the plot, exposing the lies and bringing Truth to the community ignited unity that protected them. The community left the festival feeling safer and more united than ever before.

Despite facing initial setbacks, *Heh-lel* refused to give up his cause. He devised a new strategy to further his goals - one that involved economic sabotage. He targeted several local businesses that were known to be key supporters of the unity movement, and orchestrated a series of coordinated attacks involving vandalism and theft. The timing of these attacks was highly suspicious, indicating that they were not random acts of crime but instead a deliberate attempt to undermine the movement's support base. The damage caused by these acts of sabotage was significant, and threatened to derail the unity movement's efforts towards a peaceful resolution of the ongoing conflict.

Eli and Jeremiah were known in their community as two wise and experienced prophets who had faced countless challenges in the past. However, their latest mission was perhaps the most complex and dangerous one yet. They had been entrusted with the task of uncovering a treacherous conspiracy that posed a serious threat to the peace and prosperity of their community. The web of intrigue and deception they found themselves entangled in was like nothing they had encountered before, and the stakes were higher than ever. Despite the immense pressure and danger, Eli and Jeremiah remained committed to their mission and were determined to succeed, no matter what it took.

After a long and arduous investigation, they followed the trail of clues that led them down a winding path towards a small group of individuals who had recently arrived in town. These individuals appeared to be somewhat suspicious and were found to be in possession of a number of valuable items that had been reported stolen from local businesses. Through their discernment and unwavering determination, they were able to uncover the truth and bring the perpetrators to justice.

Eli and Jeremiah were both renowned for their experience in spiritual warfare and were charged with the responsibility of investigating a series of strange occurrences that had been happening in the region.

After spending several days in prayer and meditation, they were granted a vision that revealed the true nature of the events. They discovered that a group of individuals had been hired by an unknown benefactor to carry out a series of malevolent deeds designed to disrupt the local economy and sow fear among the community. These actions included the sabotage of key infrastructure, the spread of false rumors and propaganda, and the incitement of violence between different groups of people. Eli and Jeremiah knew that it would be a challenging task to uncover the identities of those responsible and put a stop to their nefarious plans, but they were determined to do whatever it took to protect the innocent and restore peace to the land.

In a vision, Eli and Jeremiah were led to a group of conspirators who had been lured into carrying out malicious activities in exchange for lucrative rewards. The group had been engaging in covert operations for a while, causing widespread destruction of public property, spreading false rumors, and creating chaos in public spaces. Upon further investigation, it became apparent that the group's actions had severely impacted the livelihoods of local businesses and residents, leaving a trail of devastation in their wake.

Eli and Jeremiah were confronted with a complex and challenging situation. They were determined to bring the perpetrators responsible for the heinous acts to justice. They embarked on a thorough investigation, leaving no stone unturned. They meticulously gathered evidence, interviewed witnesses, and analyzed the data to reveal the truth behind the conspiracy.

For weeks, they worked tirelessly, determined to uncover the culprits behind the appalling acts. They carefully scrutinized every piece of evidence, cross-referenced every lead, and carefully scrutinized every witness account. They remained unwavering in their pursuit of justice, pushing themselves to the limit to ensure that they could identify the perpetrators.

Finally, after weeks of hard work, Eli and Jeremiah were able to uncover the conspiracy. They had identified those responsible for the heinous acts and had collected ample evidence to prove their guilt. They immediately handed over the evidence to the authorities, who promptly arrested the conspirators.

Thanks to their unwavering determination and hard work, justice was served, and the perpetrators were brought to justice.

After the community was hit by these appalling crimes, Eli took the initiative to arrange a town hall meeting. The attendees of the meeting included business owners and community leaders, who were invited to brainstorm ways to improve security measures and provide support to those who were impacted by the crimes. Eli's primary aim was to prevent any such incidents from happening in the future.

At the meeting, Eli made a courageous move by publicly exposing the connection between the series of thefts that had been taking place and Heh-lel's ongoing attempts to undermine the community's unity. The revelation was a turning point for the community, as it helped to foster an environment of mutual aid and cooperation among the community members. Eli's actions were instrumental in bringing the community members together and inspiring them to work towards the common goal of protecting their shared interests. As a result, the community's resilience was further solidified, and the members were better prepared to face any future challenges that might come their way.

The conflict between Eli and *Heh-lel* raged on, with *Heh-lel* resorting to increasingly desperate measures. In his latest scheme, he attempted to manipulate the local media to tarnish Eli's reputation. A number of news outlets were swayed by *Heh-lel's* influence and began spreading stories that cast doubt on Eli's leadership, raising suspicions about his past and motives. This underhanded tactic caused great harm to Eli's reputation and resulted in a significant setback to his cause.

These stories were carefully crafted and seeded with enough truth to be believable. They twisted Eli's previous challenges and hardships into a narrative that painted him as a controversial and divisive figure. Eli knew that this was just another attempt by *Heh-lel* to discredit him and weaken the community's resolve. But despite the challenges thrown his way, Eli remained steadfast in his commitment to the community and its well-being.

Eli, undeterred by the character assassination, invited the journalists to a public dialogue, where he openly addressed each allegation. With Jeremiah by his side, providing corroborating evidence and witness testimonials, Eli discredited the false reports. He turned the event into a lesson on the dangers of misinformation, highlighting how easily truth can be manipulated to serve the purposes of those like *Heh-lel.*

As *Sotira City* grew in unity and strength, Heh-lel's tactics became more aggressive, yet less effective. The community had learned to see through his attempts at division and to respond with an even greater commitment to solidarity and mutual support.

Through these trials, Eli not only exposed the nefarious plots of his adversary at every turn but also taught his community the power of truth, vigilance, and unity. He demonstrated that while the path to harmony is fraught with challenges, each obstacle overcome strengthens the bonds that unite. As *Sotira City* looked forward to a brighter, more united future, Eli remained a vigilant guardian, ever ready to protect the peace and prosperity they had all worked so hard to achieve. The unity they had forged was a beacon of hope, a testament to the enduring power of brotherhood against the shadows of malice and deceit.

Chapter 6: The Wisdom of Integrity

As Eli and Jeremiah continued their relentless pursuit of truth and justice, they found themselves facing a formidable adversary: Richard Greystone, the ruthless CEO of Greystone Industries. Eli and Jeremiah are two legends who have spent their entire lives fighting for the truth and justice and against the forces of corruption. They were true heroes who inspired all those around them. But their task was not easy, as they faced the unscrupulous Richard Greystone - a formidable adversary who held the reins of power in *Sotira City* with an iron grip. His empire of greed and deceit loomed over the city, casting a dark shadow of fear and intimidation.

Despite the odds stacked against them, Eli and Jeremiah never give up, and their unwavering spirit and fearlessness continue to inspire those who follow them.

Greystone's web of deceit was like a coiling serpent, slowly and steadily tightening around those who dared to challenge him, ensnaring the innocent and corrupting the hearts of the weak. The city was at his mercy, and the people lived in constant fear and uncertainty.

Yet, amidst the chaos and confusion, Eli remained unwavering in his faith and steadfast in his resolve. He refused to back down and vowed to expose the truth behind Greystone's machinations, no matter the cost.

Eli and Jeremiah were on a mission that required them to be brave and cunning. They had to infiltrate Greystone's inner circle, which was no easy feat. The two disguised themselves as allies, hoping to gain access to the information they needed to gather evidence of Greystone's many crimes.

As they delved deeper into the dangerous world of Greystone's inner circle, they encountered many obstacles. They had to navigate through a labyrinth of lies and deception, always aware that they could be discovered at any moment. Despite the many risks they faced, they remained steadfast in their determination to uncover the truth.

Greystone's loyal henchmen were always on the lookout for any signs of betrayal, and Eli and Jeremiah had to stay one step ahead of them at all times. They had to be careful not to arouse suspicion as they gathered crucial evidence that would expose Greystone's true nature.

The two protagonists remained resolute, determined to bring Greystone to justice and free the city from his tyrannical grasp. They knew the road ahead would be perilous. Still, they were willing to risk everything to restore peace and order to *Sotira City*.

The city of *Sotira City* was on the brink of destruction. Its people were held captive by fear and despair as the final battle loomed on the horizon. Eli knew the city's fate hung in the balance. Amidst the chaos, hope shone, piercing darkness and illuminating redemption's path.

By the *Power of the Spirit of Truth* and Righteousness, Eli and Jeremiah confronted Greystone, the mastermind behind the corruption plaguing the city. Fueled by courage and a strong sense of justice, they readied themselves for a battle against the dark forces that threatened to engulf them all. As the spiritual fight raged on, the very foundations of Greystone Industries began to quake, and its walls crumbled under the weight of its own corruption.

But victory was not secured by the strength of their arms or the might of their weapons. The Power of Truth, Righteousness, and Integrity triumphed over evil. Greystone fell to his knees, defeated and broken, while Eli stood tall, his spirit unbroken by the trials of the past.

As the dust settled and the smoke cleared, *Sotira City* emerged from the ashes, reborn and renewed by the *Power of Righteousness*. The city shone with a newfound light, its streets alive with worship, praise, and sounds of joy and celebration.

However, even amidst the jubilation, Eli and Jeremiah were weighed down by the cost of victory. The scars of war ran deep, and the battle had taken a toll on both their physical and emotional well-being. But the sense of triumph and liberation filled the air like a sweet fragrance that kept them going. For the people of *Sotira City*, this was not just a victory over a tyrant but a triumph of the human spirit over the forces of darkness that sought to enslave them.

As Eli surveyed the scene before him, he saw the faces of the oppressed—men, women, and children who had suffered under the yoke of oppression for far too long. But now, their chains lay broken, shattered by the Power of Truth and Righteousness.

Eli and Jeremiah had to deal with not just the physical destruction but also the emotional aftermath. Yet, they were driven by their desire to bring justice to the victims of Greystone's crimes. They collected enough evidence to bring Greystone and his minions to justice and emerged victorious from the mission.

And amidst the rubble, something miraculous began to happen. The city started to rebuild brick by brick, stone by stone. But this was no ordinary reconstruction; it was a restoration—a renewal of hope and promise that would transform *Sotira City* into a beacon of light for all the world to see. The journey was challenging, but Eli and Jeremiah were determined to see it through for the sake of the people they had fought so hard to protect.

With each passing day, the city grew stronger, its people united in their determination to forge a new future—a future built on the foundation of integrity and justice. And as the days turned into weeks, and the weeks into months, *Sotira City* emerged from the ashes like a phoenix reborn, its spirit unbroken by the trials of the past.

But even as the city flourished, Eli knew that the battle was far from over. For though Greystone had been defeated, the forces of darkness still lurked in the shadows, waiting for their chance to strike once more.

And so, with a renewed sense of purpose, Eli and Jeremiah vowed to remain vigilant—to stand guard against the ever-present threat of evil, and to ensure that the light of truth continued to shine bright in the darkness.

For they knew that as long as they remained true to their convictions, nothing could stand in their way—not even the darkest of days.

And so, as the sun set over the horizon, casting its golden rays upon the city below, Eli and Jeremiah stood side by side, their hearts filled with hope and determination.

For they knew that no matter what trials lay ahead, they would face them together, guided by the wisdom of integrity and the *Power of Righteousness.*

And as they looked out upon the city, they had fought so hard to save, they knew that their journey was far from over—but with each new day came the promise of a brighter tomorrow, filled with endless possibilities and boundless hope.

In the aftermath of the battle, as the city of *Sotira City* began to rebuild and heal, Eli and

Jeremiah turned their attention to those who had been most deeply affected by the tyranny of Greystone Industries.

They sought out the downtrodden and the oppressed, offering them solace and support in their time of need. With compassion in their hearts and a fire in their souls, they vowed to lift up the broken and the forgotten, restoring dignity and hope to those who had lost everything.

One by one, they reached out to the victims of Greystone's greed, offering them a glimmer of hope in the midst of their despair. They provided food for the hungry, shelter for the homeless, and a listening ear for those who had been silenced for too long.

Eli and Jeremiah wanted more than just address the symptoms of the problems they saw in *Sotira City*. They tried to get to the root of the issues, so they worked diligently to dismantle the systems of oppression that allowed Greystone Industries to thrive unchecked.

Their assignment and mission were not just about raising awareness of the problems in their city. They wanted to ensure that those in power were held accountable for their actions and that the most vulnerable members of their community were protected.

Through wisdom and integrity, they shone a light on the darkest corners of society, calling attention to the struggles of those who had been marginalized and silenced. Eli and the followers of *The Light*, have played a significant role in bringing critical issues to the forefront of public consciousness. By uncovering and exposing the immoral and unethical schemes and practices behind these issues, they have managed to demand and achieve much-needed change. Their tireless efforts and perseverance have not only helped to raise awareness about these issues but have also brought about positive results, leading to a better and more just society.

Their tireless efforts did not go unnoticed, inspiring many others to join their cause. Together, they worked to build a better future for all who called *Sotira City* home.

Eli and Jeremiah felt a renewed sense of purpose as they achieved victory after victory. They knew that their efforts were making a real difference in the lives of those society had forgotten.

The road ahead was long and filled with obstacles, but they faced it with courage and determination. They knew that by standing together in the power and strength of unity, they could overcome any challenge that lay in their path.

Eli and Jeremiah demonstrated that true power is not derived from wealth or influence, but rather from the strength of *The Wisdom of Integrity*. They believed in working towards a just and righteous community with unwavering perseverance, and their convictions inspire us all to strive for a world where everyone can thrive.

Eli and Jeremiah were deeply invested in the city of *Sotira City*, a city that had seen its fair share of troubled times. As the city began to rebuild itself, they decided to focus their attention on the heart of the community - the places where people came together to worship, find comfort, and connect with one another.

They embarked on a journey to visit various places of worship, including churches, synagogues, mosques, and community centers, where they interacted with spiritual leaders and congregants alike. They shared a message of hope, redemption, and the transformative power of forgiveness and reconciliation.

Drawing inspiration from the teachings of *Yeshua HaMashiach*[7], they urged all who would listen to embrace the call to love one another as *Yahweh* has loved us. They reminded the faithful of their duty to seek justice, love mercy, and walk humbly with their *Yahweh*.

Through their words, Eli and Jeremiah sought to promote a spirit of unity and compassion in the city, encouraging people of all faiths and backgrounds to come together in pursuit of a common goal - to build a better and more harmonious community for all.

Together, they prayed for healing and renewal, asking for *Yahweh's* guidance as they sought to build a community founded on principles of compassion, integrity, and faith. They prayed for unity among believers of all denominations, knowing that in their unity, they would find strength to overcome the challenges that lay ahead.

And as they prayed, they felt the presence of the Holy Spirit moving among them, filling their hearts with a sense of peace and purpose. They knew that their work was far from finished, but they also knew that with *Yahweh's* help, all things were possible.

With renewed determination, Eli and Jeremiah continued their journey, spreading seeds of hope and love wherever they went. They knew that the road ahead would be long and difficult, but they also knew that they were not alone—that *Yahweh* was with them every step of the way, guiding their path and lighting their way forward.

In their quest for justice and equality, Eli and Jeremiah turned their attention to the social structures and systems that perpetuated inequality and oppression within *Sotira City*. They recognized that true transformation required more than just individual acts of kindness—it necessitated a wholesale reimagining of society, one built on principles of fairness, equity, and compassion.

With a sense of urgency, they set out to challenge the status quo, confronting those in positions of power and privilege who benefited from the exploitation and marginalization of others. They spoke out against corruption and greed, demanding accountability and transparency in all aspects of governance and business.

Inspired by the *Divine Word of Yahweh*, Eli and Jeremiah prophesied of a world where all people were treated with dignity and respect, regardless of their race, gender, or economic status. They envisioned a community that recognized and affirmed every individual's inherent value and worth, and where justice flowed like a mighty river, washing away all stains of injustice and inequality.

This vision was based on the principle that in Christ, there is no distinction between Jew or Gentile, slave or free, male or female. This message of unity and equality still resonates powerfully with people, just as it did over 2000 years ago when it was first shared with the world.

Their efforts were met with resistance from those who sought to maintain the status quo, but Eli and Jeremiah refused to be deterred. They knew that the road to justice was fraught with obstacles, but they also knew that they served *Yahweh* who was just and righteous, and who stood with the oppressed and marginalized.

And so, they pressed on, undaunted by the challenges that lay ahead. They mobilized grassroots movements, organized peaceful protests, and lobbied government officials for policy changes that would benefit the most vulnerable members of society. They worked tirelessly to dismantle systems of oppression and to build a society where all could flourish and thrive.

As they fought for justice and equality, they drew strength from the words of the Apostle James, which calls on believers to care for the widows and orphans in their distress. They understood that true religion was not found in empty rituals or religious observances, but in acts of compassion and mercy that sought to alleviate the suffering of those in need.

And as they stood on the frontlines of the battle for justice, they knew that they were fulfilling their divine calling—to be agents of change in a world crying out for redemption. With hearts aflame with passion and purpose, they marched forward, confident in the knowledge that they served *Yahweh* who was on the side of the oppressed and who would ultimately bring about justice for all.

In their pursuit of justice and equality, Eli and Jeremiah encountered countless challenges and obstacles that tested the very core of their beings. Yet, amidst the turmoil and strife, they remained steadfast in their commitment to integrity—the unwavering adherence to moral and ethical principles that guided their every action and decision.

As they navigated the murky waters of corruption and deceit, they relied on the wisdom of King Solomon in the book of Proverbs, which teaches that integrity guards the way of the righteous but wickedness overthrows the sinner. They understood that true integrity was not merely a matter of outward appearances or empty words, but a way of life—a moral compass that directed their steps even in the darkest of times.

With each decision they made and each action they took, they sought to uphold the highest standards of honesty, transparency, and accountability, knowing that their integrity was their greatest asset in the fight against injustice and oppression.

And though they faced temptation and adversity at every turn, they refused to compromise their principles or sacrifice their integrity for the sake of expediency or personal gain. They knew that the path of righteousness was narrow and difficult, but they also knew that it was the only path worth walking.

In the face of opposition and adversity, Eli and Jeremiah stood firm, their hearts anchored in the knowledge that integrity was not just a virtue to be admired, but a weapon to be wielded against the forces of darkness and evil. They knew that in a world plagued by moral decay and ethical compromise, their commitment to integrity was a beacon of light that could guide others out of the shadows and into the light.

And so, they pressed on, undeterred by the trials and tribulations that lay ahead. They knew that the road to justice was long and arduous, but they also knew that it was paved with the stones of integrity and righteousness. With hearts aflame with passion and purpose, they marched forward, confident in the knowledge that they served *Yahweh* who valued integrity above all else, and who would honor their commitment to truth and righteousness.

As the dust settled over the ruins of Greystone Industries, and the city of *Sotira City* emerged from the shadows of despair, Eli and Jeremiah stood atop the ashes of their victory, their hearts heavy with the weight of their journey yet filled with a profound sense of purpose and fulfillment.

For they knew that their battle against the forces of darkness was not yet over—that the fight for justice and righteousness would continue until every corner of the earth was filled with the light of truth and the warmth of *Yahweh's* love.

And so, as they gazed out over the cityscape, they issued a challenge to all who would listen—a challenge to rise up and join them in their quest for justice, equality, and integrity. They called upon the people of *Sotira City* to embrace the power of truth, to reject the lies of the enemy, and to stand firm in their commitment to righteousness.

But above all, they urged them to surrender their hearts to the one true source of hope and redemption—Jesus Christ. For they knew that in Him alone lay the power to transform lives, heal broken hearts, and restore what had been lost.

And so, as the sun dipped below the horizon and darkness descended upon the city once more, Eli and Jeremiah bowed their heads in prayer, lifting up their voices to the heavens and surrendering their lives anew to the one who had called them out of darkness and into His marvelous light.

And as they whispered their final words of surrender, a sense of peace washed over them—a peace that surpassed all understanding and filled their hearts with joy unspeakable. For they knew that no matter what trials lay ahead, they walked in the light of *Yahweh's* love, and in Him, they found the strength to face whatever challenges came their way.

As they turned to leave, a single thought echoed in their minds—a thought that filled them with hope and anticipation for the future:

The battle may have been won, but the war for the soul of *Sotira City* had only just begun. And they stood ready, armed with the power of truth, the strength of integrity, and the hope of redemption, to face whatever lay ahead, knowing that with Yahweh on their side, victory was assured.

Chapter 7: Epilogue

As the sun began to set on the city of *Sotira City*, Eli and Jeremiah stood atop the highest peak, gazing out at the magnificent view before them. The sky was painted with warm hues of orange and pink, casting a golden glow over the sprawling metropolis below.

From this vantage point, the city looked almost magical. The once chaotic landscape was now bathed in a soft, romantic light, making even the most imposing skyscrapers seem welcoming and serene.

As Eli scanned the city, he felt a sense of triumph swelling in his heart. He had spent years fighting for justice and righteousness, and now, as he stood on this mountaintop, he could see the fruits of his labor. Each illuminated window in the city was a testament to the lives touched by their quest for redemption.

But as he looked closer, he could also see the shadows of injustice and despair lingering in the city. He knew their journey was far from over, and there were still battles to be fought.

Turning to Jeremiah, Eli felt grateful for his friend's companionship and support over the years. They faced countless challenges and obstacles together but always kept sight of their goal.

With determination, Eli vowed to continue the fight for *Yahweh*, no matter the cost. He knew the road ahead would be difficult, but he was confident they would prevail if they remained faithful to their calling.

As the stars twinkled in the night sky, Eli lifted his voice in a prayer of thanksgiving. He was grateful for *Yahweh's* strength and guidance in bringing them this far. And as his words echoed into the darkness, he knew their journey was far from over.

But with faith as their compass and love as their guide, they would continue to walk the path of righteousness, shining a light into the world's darkest corners. Ultimately, not the battles won, or the enemies defeated mattered most, but the hearts touched and the lives changed along the way.

As long as they persevered, Eli knew they would leave a legacy of hope and redemption that would endure for generations.

Glossary

[1]Sotira City

"*Sotira City*" translates to " *City of Salvation*" *in Hebrew*, where "*Sotira*" means salvation *(from the Greek word "σωτηρία" for salvation).* "*Salvation*" in Hebrew is "ישועה" (*Yeshu'ah*). Please keep in mind the following text, which aims to convey the essence of "Sotira City". The city represents a sanctuary or a place of safety where people can seek refuge from danger or harm. It evokes a sense of hope, deliverance, and renewal, as it is a chance for redemption and a new beginning. The language used in the description is descriptive, evocative, and emotionally resonant, in order to create a vivid and immersive experience for the reader.

[2]Eli

"*Eli*" is a Hebrew name that translates to "*my Yahweh.*" It is a short and poignant name, often used both as a personal name and as a component in longer names. In the Bible, Eli is notably the name of a priest and judge who serves as a mentor to the prophet Samuel. The name is frequently used to express a *personal relationship or closeness to Yahweh*, reflecting a deep spiritual connection.

³Jeremiah

"Jeremiah" is a name of Hebrew origin, derived from *"Yirmeyahu"* (ירמיהו) which means *"Yahweh has exalted"* or *"appointed by Yahweh."* Jeremiah is a significant figure in the Hebrew Bible, known as one of the major prophets. The Book of Jeremiah contains his prophecies and portrays his mission to warn Judah of its impending destruction by Babylon if they did not turn back to Yahweh. Jeremiah's life and prophetic ministry are marked by his deep emotions, struggles with despair, and his unwavering commitment to delivering Yahweh's message despite intense persecution.

⁴Heh-lel

The term *"Heh-lel"* (הֵילֵל), which is often transliterated as *"Helel"* or *"Hêlēl"*, is a Hebrew word meaning *"shining one"* or *"light-bearer."* It appears in the Hebrew Bible in Isaiah 14:12, where it is used to describe a fallen morning star. This passage is often interpreted as referring to a Babylonian king who fell from power, but it has also been traditionally linked to the *Christian concept of Lucifer or Satan,* due to the association with a celestial being who fell from heaven. The passage and the term itself have been subjects of much theological and literary interpretation.

[5]Sarah

The name *"Sarah"* is of Hebrew origin and means *"princess"* or *"noblewoman."* It is derived from the Hebrew word "שָׂרָה" (*Sārāh*).

[6]Uriel

The name Uriel is of Hebrew origin and carries a rich biblical and angelic association. In Hebrew, Uriel is written as אוריאל and is derived from two Hebrew elements: אור (Or) meaning "light" or "flame," and אל (El) meaning "God." Therefore, the name Uriel can be interpreted as *"God is my light"* or *"Light of God."*

Uriel is one of the archangels in Jewish and Christian traditions, though mentioned more prominent in apocryphal texts rather than the canonical scriptures of these religions. In texts where mentioned, Uriel is often depicted as a figure of wisdom and enlightenment, one who illuminates our path with truth and divine knowledge.

This name carries connotations of illumination, both literal and metaphorical, implying that the bearer of the name or the entity it describes is someone who brings light and clarity, much like a beacon of divine wisdom and guidance.

⁷Yeshua HaMashiach

In Hebrew, the name Jesus Christ is typically rendered as "ישו המשיח" (Yeshua HaMashiach). Here, "ישו" (Yeshua) is the Hebrew form of the name Jesus, and "המשיח" (HaMashiach) means "the Messiah," which translates to "the Anointed One."

⁸Yahweh

In Hebrew, the word for God is often written as "אלוהים" (Elohim). This is a plural form, but it is commonly used in a singular sense when referring to the God of Israel. Another common name for God, particularly in a more personal and sacred context, is the Tetragrammaton "יהוה" (YHWH), often vocalized as "**Yahweh**" or "Jehovah" in English, though traditionally not pronounced aloud by observant Jews, who instead say "Adonai" meaning "Lord" when reading aloud.

[9]*Jezebel*

Jezebel was a Phoenician princess who married King Ahab of Israel and is described in the Old Testament, specifically in the Books of Kings. She is portrayed as a woman of great beauty and charm, but with a manipulative and deceitful nature. Jezebel was known for her rebelliousness against God, idol worship, and disregard for moral principles.

The term "*Jezebel Spirit*" refers to a person or influence that embodies certain negative traits or behaviors in a contemporary context. This spirit is often associated with a domineering and controlling personality, a tendency to manipulate and deceive others, and a disregard for moral and ethical standards. Individuals who exhibit the "*Jezebel Spirit*" are often adept at creating chaos and confusion in their personal and professional relationships, and they can be very difficult to deal with.

The "*Jezebel Spirit*" is a negative force that seeks to undermine God's plan and lead people astray. It is often associated with targeting Christian leaders.

The most effective way to combat the "*Jezebel Spirit*" is to stay vigilant, remain true to your faith in Jesus Christ, and meditate on The Word of God, especially during times of adversity.

The "*Jezebel Spirit*" is manipulative and controlling spirit that can be encountered in various aspects of life. The best way to deal with such a person that manifests this spirit is to remain vigilant and stay true to your faith in Jesus Christ. This involves studying and meditating on The Word of God, especially in the face of adversity. It is important to remember that God is always present, and He is willing to guide and comfort you through difficult situations. By relying on your faith and seeking God's help, you can effectively counteract the negative influence of the *"Jezebel Spirit."* Additionally, it is essential to maintain healthy boundaries and avoid being drawn into the manipulative behavior of such individuals. Remember, God's love is unconditional, and by staying true to your faith, you can overcome any obstacle that comes your way.

Here are some characteristics and tactics often attributed to the *Jezebel Spirit*:

1. **Manipulation**: The *Jezebel Spirit* is often said to manipulate others for personal gain or to achieve power. This manipulation can be subtle, involving psychological tactics like gaslighting, lying, or using emotional guilt to control others.

2. **Seduction**: This doesn't necessarily refer only to sexual seduction but can include any form of luring individuals away from their ethical beliefs or duties. It involves persuading others to compromise their principles or loyalties, often slowly and almost imperceptibly.

3. **Intimidation**: The spirit uses fear to intimidate others. Those influenced by this spirit may threaten or coerce others to enforce obedience or silence criticism.

4. **Domination**: Linked closely with manipulation, this trait involves a strong desire to control situations and people, particularly in leadership or influential positions. It involves a disregard for the freedom and rights of others, preferring instead to dominate and dictate.

5. **Falsehood**: The *Jezebel Spirit* is often associated with falsehood, both in terms of spreading lies and in deceitful behavior. This can involve false accusations, twisting facts, or presenting a false persona to the world to hide one's true intentions.

6. **Undermining Authority**: It often works to undermine legitimate authority and to disrespect or subvert established structures of power, particularly those that promote justice and righteousness.

7. **Spiritual Deception**: Perhaps one of its most dangerous aspects, the *Jezebel Spirit* might also work to lead people away from true spiritual commitments and beliefs, often promoting idolatry or other forms of spiritual compromise.

8. **Fostering Discord**: This spirit seeks to create divisions and strife within communities, particularly within churches or families, by setting people against each other, fostering unhealthy competition, and encouraging conflicts.

The concept of the *Jezebel Spirit* is used in Christian teaching and counseling to help identify and combat these negative behaviors and influences. It is seen as a call for vigilance and spiritual maturity to resist such influences and to uphold integrity, transparency, and fidelity to one's faith and moral principles.

About The Author

Eric Cooper is a prophetic leader, mentor, and teacher passionate about helping people discover their purpose in Christ. With over four decades of experience, Eric's leadership style uniquely blends wisdom, prophetic insight, warmth, and compassion. He has empowered countless individuals to unlock their potential and positively impact the world. We hope Eric's book has inspired you and provided valuable insights.

Author Link: amazon.com/author/abovethesun
Personal Website: ericcooper.com
Publisher Website: abovethesun.ca

For more information, or to book an event, contact:
contact@abovethesun.ca
https://www. abovethesun.ca

Our Books

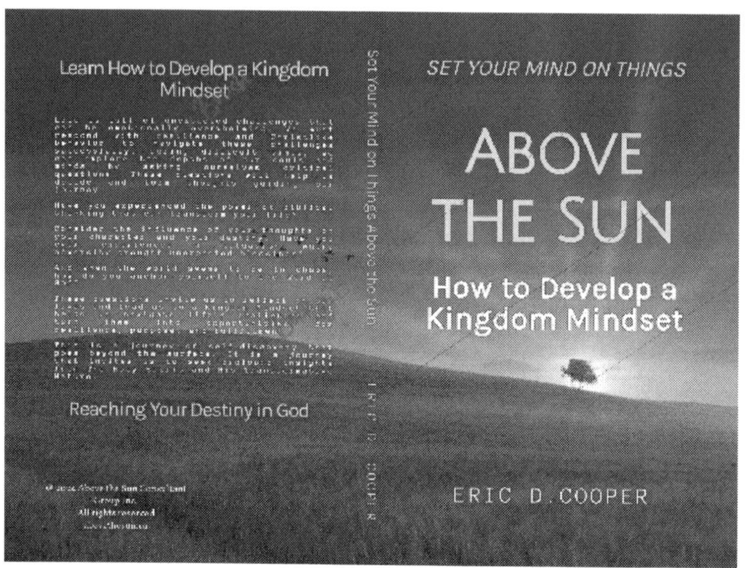

Set Your Mind on Things Above the Sun
How to Develop a Kingdom Mindset

In a world filled with distractions and challenges, how do you maintain a Kingdom mindset and walk in the supernatural power of the Holy Spirit? It all starts with where you focus your attention and what you choose to empower in your life.

Join author Eric D. Cooper on a transformative journey into the depths of intentional focus and spiritual empowerment. In *"Set Your Mind on Things Above the Sun,"* you'll discover the profound impact of aligning your thoughts with Yahweh's wisdom and purpose. No longer will you feel overwhelmed by the chaos of everyday life. You will learn to navigate challenges with confidence and clarity.

Through practical insights and timeless Biblical principles, Cooper equips readers with the tools needed to break free from self-centered tendencies and embrace a life of purpose and fulfillment. This isn't just another self-help guide — it's a blueprint for living a well-lived life rooted in Kingdom principles.

As you turn each page, you'll uncover the keys to strengthening your connection with Yahweh and unlocking your true destiny. With each revelation, you'll be empowered to make spirit-led choices that shape your future and impact the world around you.

Prepare to be captivated by the awesome power of Yahweh's presence as you embark on this enlightening journey. Let ***"Set Your Mind on Things Above the Sun"*** guide you as you uncover the wisdom, resilience, and destiny that await you. It's time to step into the fullness of who you were created to be.

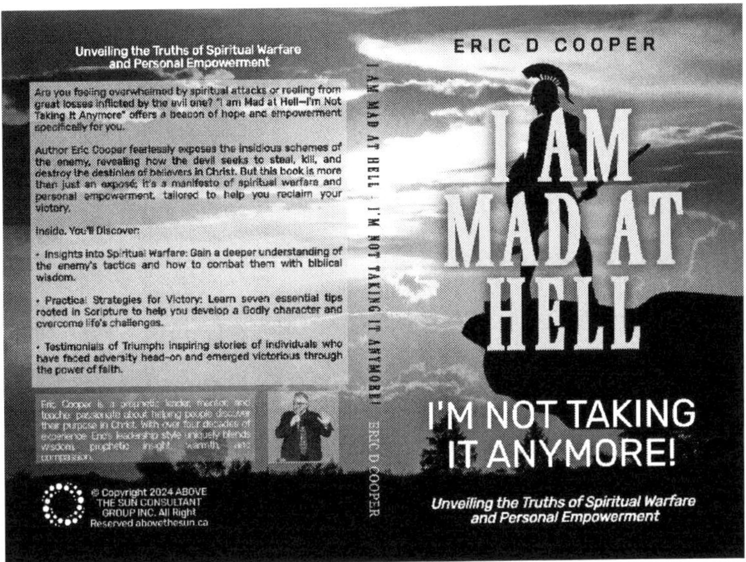

I am Mad at Hell—I'm Not Taking It Anymore

Unveiling the Truths of Spiritual Warfare

and Personal Empowerment

Are you feeling overwhelmed by spiritual attacks or reeling from great losses inflicted by the evil one? ***"I am Mad at Hell—I'm Not Taking It Anymore"*** offers a beacon of hope and empowerment specifically for you. Author

Eric Cooper fearlessly exposes the insidious schemes of the enemy, revealing how the devil seeks to steal, kill, and destroy the destinies of believers in Christ. But this book is more than just an exposé; it's a manifesto of spiritual warfare and personal empowerment, tailored to help you reclaim your victory.

Inside, You'll Discover:

- **Insights into Spiritual Warfare**: Gain a deeper understanding of the enemy's tactics and how to combat them with Biblical wisdom.

- **Practical Strategies for Victory**: Learn seven essential tips rooted in Scripture to help you develop a Godly character and overcome life's challenges.

- **Testimonials of Triumph**: Inspiring stories of individuals who have faced adversity head-on and emerged victorious through the power of faith.

Whether you're battling personal struggles, facing spiritual attacks, or grappling with losses inflicted by the evil one, ***"I am Mad at Hell—I'm Not Taking It Anymore"*** is your roadmap to victory. Join the ranks of those who refuse to be defeated and discover the transformative power of faith and resilience.

Take the first step towards reclaiming your destiny and defeating the forces of darkness. Order your copy today and embark on a journey of spiritual awakening, personal growth, and unshakeable faith.

Restoration Journey

A Daily Guide to Rebuilding Your Relationship with God through the Psalms and Proverbs

Embark on a transformative journey of restoration and renewal with **"Restoration Journey:** *A Daily Guide to Rebuilding Your Relationship with God through the Psalms and Proverbs."*

In a world filled with distractions and chaos, finding solace and connection with the divine can seem like an uphill battle. Yet, within the timeless wisdom of the Psalms and Proverbs lies a roadmap for rebuilding and deepening our relationship with the Almighty.

Each day offers a fresh opportunity to draw closer to God, to rediscover His presence, and to experience the profound joy of walking in His ways. Through this daily guide, you will embark on a soul-stirring expedition through the sacred texts of Psalms and Proverbs, immersing yourself in their rich insights and timeless truths.

From the heartfelt cries of the Psalms to the practical wisdom of Proverbs, you will find guidance, comfort, and inspiration for every step of your journey. Each day's reading is carefully curated to align with the rhythms of life, offering wisdom and encouragement for the challenges you face and the joys you celebrate.

As you delve into the depths of scripture, you will uncover the keys to healing, restoration, and spiritual growth. Through reflection questions, prayers, and practical applications, you will be empowered to apply these timeless truths to your daily life, cultivating a deeper intimacy with God and a renewed sense of purpose and direction.

Whether you are seeking to reignite your passion for prayer, to find solace in times of trial, or to cultivate a heart of wisdom and discernment, **_"Restoration Journey"_** offers a guiding light to illuminate your path. Join us on this sacred pilgrimage of the soul and discover the abundant blessings that await as you rebuild your relationship with God, one day at a time.

NAVIGATING
STORMS &
KEEPING
Faith

ERIC D. COOPER

ABOVE THE SUN
CONSULTANT GROUP

40490348R00081